For my darling Evie

The Hidden Gateway

and the Golden Labrador

David Lydiat

CONTENTS

The Hidden Gateway and the Golden Labrador
The First Story in the Hidden Gateway series

Written by David Lydiat
lydiatbooks@gmail.com

Cover and book illustrations by Lawrence McClelland
lawrencemcclellandart.co.uk

CHAPTER ONE –
AT THE PALACE

As the little girl gazed upwards at the magnificent pastel building with its protruding spires, glorious sculptures and tranquil fountains, Evie couldn't help but wonder what the Princess inside the Great Palace was doing today.

She was standing so close that she could reach out and touch the cold stone wall surrounding the palace and yet Evie always felt it represented a world set far apart from her own.

Despite this, the girl in the pink jacket was upbeat and for a very good reason; leaving her own house in the town, even for just a short while, felt like freedom to Evie. Mother said she couldn't stay still and had too much energy.

She was an exceptionally bright and excitable girl, and walks with her father and her beloved Labrador Rafa meant one thing - an adventure!

On her walks Evie would often dream about countless fairy tales, inspired by age old stories of princesses in faraway lands.

Evie wished she was a Princess. She wished it more than anything.

Even more so today as the three of them were going on her favourite walk of all - around the gleaming emerald lake and to the woods of the Great Palace. The Spring sunshine made the air come alive as Blackbirds, Robins and Skylarks all sang together in chorus. Evie knew the palace grounds had become the only sanctuary for local birds in the Shire these days; the Town's spread was ever increasing. Hearing bird song lifted her spirits.

Despite it only being mid-Spring the midday sun would soon be overwhelming. The ground was hard and dry underfoot as it had not rained for three weeks. This most recent heatwave still had a month to last, but it did not stop them using their allotted time for outdoor exercise.

"Father can you hear that Lark? Over there, I see it!" Evie shouted with joy spotting the small bird hovering higher and higher over the vibrant green grass.

Evie noticed her father's face light up, but all too briefly. She could tell the town was growing more and more dispiriting for him.

Evie's make-believe imagination was no longer shared by Father. He had stopped pretending to be a king or a knight; Father always seemed far too distracted now for playing games like that, which had made Evie sad. But she hoped the Dahlia tuba in her pocket would cheer him up. The little girl had waited all winter to plant it and now she just had to find the right spot at the palace grounds.

If they were really lucky, when visiting the palace, they would see the last Red Deer stag and hind in the whole of the Shire, but that had become an increasingly rare spectacle these days as green shire transformed to grey town. During

Father's lessons he had taught her about the hedgehogs that used to roam here in their dozens before she was born and he even thought he had spotted a badger once. They were all gone now of course. Regardless, to be away from the town for their daily exercise was liberating.

Rafa always led the way, his wet nose sniffing the ground as he moved. He seemed more lion than dog to Evie with his tremendous paws and long fur. At least, from the old videos on her screen she thought he resembled a lion.

Despite the obvious difference in size between the pair, Evie's canine companion was her best friend and protector. They loved playing games together and they both had matching and striking golden-blonde hair.

Father was struggling to keep up today; he was coughing as they made their way through the town. Thankfully it had eased up once they reached the palace grounds. He blamed it on the latest factory starting its furnace.

"If only we could have our time again, people would do things differently." Father would often mutter.

Rafa had the tendency to disappear into the distance on walks around the palace. But the giant dog would always reappear again, almost out of thin air it seemed.

They continued their journey, down to the

bottom of the hill, until they reached the edge of the palace wood. Its dark trees imposingly rose above them and cast a looming shadow. Other children might have thought twice about entering, but not Evie, it was just another adventure and she couldn't wait to explore her enchanted forest, to smell its rich scents and to feel the natural touch of the leaves – none of these pleasantries could be experienced near her home.

Rafa seemed to go the same way every time. As though he was late the Golden Labrador moved with purpose today. Her dog darted this way and that, behind the trees, moving further and further into the distance at haste. Come to think of it the Lab hadn't seemed himself this morning she had observed. Where was he going? Evie wished he would stay close.

Before long Evie and Father found themselves running after him, calling out.

"Raf, come back!" Evie shouted as loud as her little voice could muster.

But Rafa didn't look back.

Evie was worried, something was wrong.

They came to a brook, though its placid water curling through the woodland had run dry, and then passed the oaks, presently they glimpsed a sight of familiar golden fur in a clearing… something had made him pause.

Evie had to hold her father's hand as they made

their way through the dense flora to the clearing.

"Take care darling" Father whispered, desperately trying to avoid the thorns, he could sense something was wrong too.

As they emerged from the woodland, Rafa was stood before them in front of a mysteriously placed gate. It soon became apparent that this was indeed the strangest and yet most wonderful hidden gateway Evie had ever seen, in fact it was the only hidden gateway she had ever seen! Made of beautifully carved wood; it shone in the sunlight.

The gate was engraved in a writing that was not familiar to the little girl. What's more it was standing solitary in the middle of the clearing, attached to no fence nor obvious barrier. Just layers of vines, weeds and moss growing over the wood hinting at how long the gateway had stood there.

The Labrador took one longing look at Evie and pushed his way through the entrance of the gateway… suddenly he disappeared.

CHAPTER TWO –
THROUGH THE
GATEWAY

Evie could not believe her eyes, she must have imagined what she had just seen.

Father gripped her hand tightly. "That can't be possible…"

He had seen it too, the Golden Labrador had walked through the entrance of the hidden gateway but did not come through the other side.

Slowly father and daughter made their way to where Rafa had stood and peered through the wooden gate. All they could see was the other side of the clearing and the cherry blossom trees beyond it.

"We have to find him, we cannot leave Rafa." Evie cried.

"We will." Father tried to sound confident, though he knew their allocated time away from the town was running out.

He stepped forward and cautiously pushed against the gateway but it would not move. Father tried pushing harder… still nothing.

He then leaned against the gate putting all his (admittedly slender) weight against the wooden barrier. Yet the gateway was still.

Father was getting annoyed now and began shoving furiously, but it still didn't budge. "Darn thing."

He walked around to inspect the other side.

As he did so Evie, who had been transfixed by the hidden gateway, pressed her hand against it and was surprised by the smooth, cool texture. The wooden frame began to swing open; she had a strange feeling that it would.

"Father I've opened it!" she exclaimed proudly.

"I must have loosened it!" Father said hopefully.

They held hands again, took a deep breath and walked through. As they did so there was the strongest smell of frankincense and a bright light momentarily blinded them, but they kept advancing forward.

In the blink of an eye they were standing by a grand Common Ash tree next to a large running river curling away as far as they could see. The water was clear and fresh. So much so Evie could spot a group of Perch swimming downstream beneath the current.

Evie and Father looked around in bewilderment. A vast green natural landscape stood before them. They had never seen anything like it.

They both instinctively took slow, deep breaths in order to appreciate the fresh atmosphere surrounding them. The oxygen which filled their lungs was like a medicine to the town's polluted streets.

A huge forest stood way out to the west, to the north, mountains with tips of snow glistened on the horizon, to the East the river dominated, and when they looked south, just ahead of them they saw open fields with an abundance of daffodils, primrose, charlock and other flowers. On closer inspection there were bees and butterflies hovering everywhere. Evie had only ever seen Brimstones at the palace, but never this much colour and variety.

They looked at each other in disbelief, this was the most magnificent place Evie had ever set foot in. More sensational than she imagined from the bedtime stories of the Shire that her parents recited; reminiscing from their own childhoods. How the world had changed since then. Now it was Evie's world that had been turned upside down - but how did they even arrive in this dreamland she wondered?

Presently they heard a soft trickling sound in the river. There, gliding across the water, was a boat, its size was considerable despite its graceful drift with a vast white sail being pushed by a gentle wind. Evie recognised the striking wood the hull was made out of – it was the same as the hidden gateway.

It reached the bank in front of Father and Evie with a soft thud.

And as if this day could not become any stranger, out of the boat jumped their dog Rafa. Only he looked different, his coat shined more golden than ever and he appeared much taller.

Evie looked him up and down; the Labrador was wearing a crown, as golden as he was. The dog looked resplendent.

"Am I dreaming Father?" Evie asked

"We both must be." Father claimed.

Then two by two other animals followed from the boat. Evie recognised them from her screen time lessons; foxes, badgers, hares, rabbits and finally a little white mouse.

"Evie I am glad you are here, our world is under grave threat."

The little girl nearly fell over, for it was not her father who had uttered those words, but her Golden Labrador Rafa.

CHAPTER THREE –
THE GOLDEN LABRADOR
AND THE PROPHECY

"…we need your help" he repeated.

Evie stood, open mouthed, in astonishment.

In these most recent moments, her very own pet Labrador had been talking to her in a rich, warm voice that raised the hairs on the back of her neck on end.

The dog did look like a colossal lion now and towered over the little girl. His cavernous green eyes fixated on hers.

A silence passed between animals and humans, all congregated in a circle.

She finally managed to speak; "We want to help, but first please, tell us, how can you talk and where are we?"

Evie's father still hadn't moved an inch during the whole time.

"Allow me to start from the beginning" The Golden Labrador started courteously. "You stand in the realm of Nineveh; this is nature's world as it was intended. Animals, birds, fish, reptiles, insects, trees and flowers live and thrive here."

"It is our refuge, no animal is mute in this world like your own." The little white mouse interrupted, much to the delight of Evie, who held out her hand for it. The mouse felt reassured in her presence and gladly clambered onto her hand. Only now did she appreciate his striking red eyes.

The girl began very gently to stroke its white fur up and down, which made the mouse laugh.

"That tickles" he squeaked.

The Labrador continued his story. "This haven for nature has existed since the creation of your own realm; many of our kind came here when they were forced to flee your world as mankind built up its towns. Too many did not escape."

"The Golden Labrador is a Realm Mover; one of the chosen twelve who can move between worlds. This power was gifted by the Ancient One." Mouse explained proudly. Evie's eyes lit up; she always knew her dog was special.

The golden canine continued, "Evie there is a reason I have led you here; the gateway was about to shut, Nineveh's first full moon was coming to an end, and our situation grows dire."

"But why me? I'm just a little girl, how can I help you?" Evie asked.

Rafa turned to the other animals, and one of the badgers stepped forward carrying something.

"This ancient scroll was discovered by the rabbits" Rafa explained "it is thousands of years old Evie."

"We were digging a new burrow when we found it you see." Mrs Rabbit clarified "We were forced to move home for our own safety."

As Badger slowly unravelled the delicate but ragged parchment Evie saw a great many drawings and words; it was inscribed in the same style of writing as was on the hidden gateway in the palace woods. She looked closer and amongst the tears, could just make out an illustrated story appearing to show nature being destroyed; just like it had been at home.

As she continued to study the ripped scroll (which appeared to be decomposing, it was missing segments and was therefore admittedly difficult to make out) she noticed an image of a girl. Her heart skipped a beat; the drawing was an uncanny resemblance of herself. Or so she thought. Though the girl was drawn holding a shield like a brave knight of old, Evie couldn't remember ever having held a shield before!

"What does that say?" she asked pointing to the text under the drawing.

The Golden Labrador drew his breath and eloquently delivered part of the prophecy.

"We cannot be truly certain about the meaning of the ancient text, but we believe that the Scroll reads as follows:

'Upon Nineveh's darkest hour,
Look to the daughter of another world
Who raises her shield to empower
Our kindred nation to rebuild.'"

Rafa paused and waited for a reaction.

Evie looked impressed by her poetic canine, Mouse even started to applaud enthusiastically as though he had just listened to a sonnet. When the little rodent realised he was the only one clapping, his little smile revealed his embarrassment and the applause quickly stopped.

But it was Father who moved forward to take the scroll and read it for himself – though Evie was quite sure he couldn't understand the strange text.

Father asked why the animals could not be certain what was written and scoffed when they admitted some of the words were missing due to the condition of the scroll. Moreover, the writing that was used was so old, much of its meaning had long since been forgotten.

"So, if I understand this situation correctly Raf, you brought Evie here to…" he paused "…fight for you? Based on this silly rhyme!? And even then you are not sure that is what is said here… I have never heard such nonsense." Father flung the scroll to the ground dismissively, another piece of parchment broke away and pirouetted in the leisurely breeze before elegantly brushing the grass as it came to a stop.

"That's Prince Rafa to you old boy and you will do well to remember it around here." Fox snapped sternly.

"You're a Prince?!" Evie shouted excitedly.

"This is the ancient prophecy, it cannot be undone." Rafa calmly replied to Father. "Look at the image and tell me that is not your daughter."

The resemblance suddenly dawned on Father, though he tried not to show it. "I will not allow you to put Evie in harm's way. And besides, we must return home soon, our allocated time is nearly over."

"Time stands still in your world while you reside here; this is how I could come to Nineveh and return without you knowing. I am afraid you cannot go back now until the next moon of Nineveh opens the gateway. So you will both need to follow me, on board my boat. I need to show you something important." The Golden Labrador declared.

CHAPTER FOUR –
VOYAGE INTO THE DEEP
FOREST

They had sailed down river and through ageless forest for what seemed like days, much to Evie's enjoyment. Though in this strange new world it felt impossible to keep track of time.

She gazed upon the abundant greenery before her and saw more wildlife than she had ever seen in her whole life up until that very moment. The Realm of Nineveh dwarfed the little girl and she had no idea how she was going to be able to 'empower it' as the prophecy scroll suggested.

Evie also spent the voyage enjoying the company of the animals, particularly Mouse who had kindly given her raspberries and blackberries to eat which were refreshing and sweet to taste.

Father was a little distant, still sceptical and half expecting to wake up from this fantastical dream. Meanwhile Fox didn't seem too keen on him.

Rafa guided them through the realm of Nineveh on their journey: the enclaves, the nature, the history. But he did not broach the subject of whatever it was that was threatening this incredible land. At least not yet.

The animals navigated the boat towards the bank, deep in the forest, a large fallen tree made the landing ground. Perched on top of it, waiting patiently for them, was a barn owl. With captivating white and brown feathers and deep black eyes like the bottom of a well. She looked as wise as owls were always depicted in the nursery rhymes that Mother read to Evie before bedtime.

Alongside the owl was a stag and a hind, magnificent Red Deer. Powerful yet elegant, almost regal. Evie recognised them straight away, though she had not seen them for some time.

Father seemed excited when Evie pointed out they were the deer from the palace grounds – the last in the Shire. "So this is why we can no longer find you on our walks. You live here now."

"We could not risk staying a moment longer." Said the Stag.

"Prince Rafa led us to safety, and just in time too." added the Hind.

All of the animals disembarked, except the Labrador.

"Evie will remain with my friends, she is safe here. Father there is something that you need to see."

Father embraced Evie tightly and reluctantly climbed back into the boat. She watched, concerned as they both drifted down the river and for a brief moment felt very alone.

"Come with us little one" Owl hooted.

"We have so much to show you" said Mouse, who had taken a fondness to Evie ever since she had stroked his fur in the most agreeable way.

The animals walked (or flew!) with the girl through the forest. The woodland was so dense she could only just see the glimmers of the blue sky through the tops of the trees.

In the town it was the tower buildings that blocked the sky. The air was dirty and the noise was overbearing, with the people always rushing this way and that.

Here the air was fresh, the only noise was a requiem of birdsong.

Evie saw plants, shrubs and trees of all kinds. And some, she did not recognise from her lessons. She did have a few seedlings and saplings in the secret 'garden' in her bedroom. But there is only so much that will grow in a few old pots in unnatural light. That is why Evie always felt the palace grounds were the best place for them once green shoots appeared.

"Can I collect some seeds, oh please may I?" She asked excitedly, thinking about all the new flowers that could be grown.

"Of course but take only what you need. Remember child, you reap what you sow here." Owl advised sagely.

"And what about what we need Owl?" Fox said disdainfully "This girl is yet to prove herself."

"Do you doubt the prophecy Fox?" Owl questioned.

"It is difficult to have faith in something you have not yet seen." Fox replied.

"That is why it is called faith." Owl pointed out.

To prevent a quarrel, a test was devised by Fox

for Evie to solve before she would be permitted to harvest the seeds.

With a cunning smirk Fox paced back and forth in front of the girl and the others and he asked this riddle:

"I am want, I am greed
I am pest, I am disease
I am fear, I bring tears
I am darkness, smothering, all consuming
What am I?"

Evie wasn't sure she understood, but set to work deciphering the words. Muttering to herself and scratching her head hoping for inspiration. She looked up at Owl who was perched in a nearby Oak and raised an eyebrow back at the girl.

Mouse has his hand raised wanting to answer, but a stern look from Fox saw the little white rodent slowly lower his arm and look the other way.

Then it came to Evie: "I am human."

"And don't forget it." said Fox disappointingly as he slunk away through the trees.

The watching animals cheered and congratulated the little girl. Then they set about helping Evie to collect – a fair proportion – of seeds and herbal remedies. Deep yellow Marigold and bright white Elderflower amongst others were carefully gathered. Owl explained that these could cure many ailments.

Evie marvelled as her collection grew.

Mouse was particularly productive, his small size and speed making him ideal for moving from one plant to the next.

In appreciation, Evie reached into her pocket and pulled out the Dahlia tuba she had intended for the palace, "I want you to have this." she held it out for Mouse and a little tear rolled down his cheek.

"Thank you, I will treasure the flower that will grow from it." Mouse said gratefully.

He planted it, and within moments dark green shoots emerged before Evie's eyes. Then from the foliage, blazing orange petals with pale tips, around black centres. The Dahlia proudly displayed before them.

"That is incredible" exclaimed Evie, though Mouse was unsure if she referred to the beauty of the Bishop of Oxford flower or the speed in which it surfaced.

"Nature grows quickly in Nineveh, particularly flora tenderly cared for." Owl revealed.

Evie was fast becoming enchanted by this foreign and wonderful land.

Later, once they had finished, she put her cuttings and seeds into a special satchel that Mrs Badger had made for her, with a green 'E' embroidered on the front.

Suddenly Owl flew down silently before her

"come child, some friends of ours want to meet you."

Evie was led through thick shrub, her footsteps crackling on the leaves that had fallen the previous Autumn.

Eventually she reached a descent and beyond it a clearing surrounded by trees of all kinds on raised ground. They walked further to a clearing which was carpeted by sensational clusters of Bluebells. Standing before her were hundreds of animals as far as her eyes could see.

"They have travelled far to see you little one." explained Owl.

Evie spotted bears, wolves, boars, bulls, wildcats, swans, pheasants, kites, merlin… and more besides standing and perched side-by-side.

It was quite a sight for the little girls to behold, not for an age had such a gathering of animals taken place.

"These were the animals of my country, before mankind drove them away" Evie realised.

Suddenly she jumped as they all began cheering at her. The noise was deafening, but Evie beamed a smile and waved though was unsure what warranted such a greeting.

"You bring them hope." said Owl.

"Remember I was friends with you first!" exclaimed Mouse.

Evie and the animals then enjoyed a feast of the forest which lasted long into the night. Owl and the others showed the little girl the value of keeping the seeds of the fruits and vegetables they ate. There were berries of all kinds and colours, juicy red and yellow tomatoes, green apples and pears, peas, runner beans, mushrooms and sweet corn. All washed down with fresh spring water. The meal was delicious and organic. Satisfied, Evie began to realise that it didn't taste like the food back in the town.

Later, the kept seeds were then scattered onto fertile soil and watered, within moments green shoots began to emerge again before Evie's eyes. At that moment she understood the meaning of what Owl had told her earlier; you do reap what you sow in Nineveh.

As the evening wore on the younger animals, Evie and Mouse laughed and played and were merry. They sang songs and danced around fire torches.

The girl's blonde hair swung back and forth widely as she skipped one way and then another. During these moments there were no worries to weigh her down, just excitement and fun.

The elder animals however, such as Bear and the Red Deer, seemed preoccupied; they were deep in conversation, whispering undertones about what was to come and in speculation for their absent leader.

The party was abruptly halted by a loud tapping sound. Evie turned and looked up to see Owl, perched near the top of a grand Chestnut tree holding a smooth pebble in her sharp talons. The other animals began gathering together in circles around the tree. The young girl sat crossed legged amongst them eager to find out what was going to happen next.

"Owl is going to tell us all a tale." Mouse whispered to her.

The white and brown barn owl cleared her throat and recounted a story from long ago which began in a garden set in a valley below the stars.

This garden was vast with everything one could ever imagine growing and living there; everything that any creature could ever need. But one day, very suddenly, the harmony of all the creatures in the garden was broken. A dark shadow grew over the land and they turned against one another with envious thoughts; despite each having plenty.

All the creatures agreed that they could no longer live together and had no choice but to leave the garden and seek out new homes where they could dwell amongst themselves. They created doorways to keep the others out. The common language and way of life was eventually forgotten.

And so a wondrous and unique place - the garden - was lost forever to each one of them.

Whispers gradually built up below Owl as the animals pondered the meaning of the story and the lessons that they could all learn. Evie wondered if the story was true or a work of fiction.

CHAPTER FIVE –
THE GREY THREAT

The voyage along the river with Rafa felt surreal to Father. Here he stood with his pet Labrador who had been by his side since he was a puppy. Even back then he was big. His large paws clumsily padded around the house exploring his new home.

Father enjoyed the memory. "Why haven't you told us about all of this before?" he asked as the river pulled the boat along in its current. The time he had spent in the vessel, and being away from his daughter, made Father uneasy and impatient.

The Golden Labrador stared ahead into the distance and took a deep breath, "I am mute in your world. Only now that the scroll was found and the prophecy revealed at this desperate time could I show you. Furthermore, the other animals could not risk humans in Nineveh, this is their sanctuary... at least it was."

Father noticed the lush clear water had turned a murky black, no fish swam in this part of the river. Then, up ahead an extensive shadowy building appeared.

"We travel on foot from here" Rafa said ominously.

Father would have leapt at the chance to leave the boat a little earlier, but the recent change in atmosphere sent a chill down his spine – why did it feel like such a warning?

The pair silently made their way from the bank, taking care to keep to the shadows that the woods afforded them. An eerie quiet enveloped the companions; Father realised there was no wildlife amongst the trees in this part of Nineveh.

After a while, at the Labrador's instruction, they began crawling up a small ridge, which revealed a gloomy vision. Both stayed low so they would not be spotted.

It became clear that the building was a colossal and dreary factory, its chimney billowed black smoke, a giant water wheel churned through the river spewing black tar into the already tainted water. All of the trees in the immediate area had been felled, all that remained of them were scars of short stumps sticking out of the ground. It was an image of devastation.

Mysterious figures lurked, stomping in and out of the building, some carrying huge sacks of timber, others carrying sacks with tails hanging out of the end. Father could not bear to think what was happening here.

"They are destroying our world, one tree at a time, one habitat at a time, one life at a time." Rafa explained with a heavy heart.

Father managed to catch a good look at the shadowy figures. They had familiar features, walking upright on two legs with two long overgrown arms and hands. Though their faces were somewhat different to his own; cold, expressionless, hairier. The hair which covered the majority of their bodies was a bleak grey and they were large hulks of men.

"I am sorry" said Father.

"You know how this ends, they won't rest until the whole of Nineveh looks like this, becomes like your town. My friends are in danger, but everything you once held dear can still be saved." Rafa spoke passionately.

Suddenly the Grey Creatures began to gather together. Then another emerged from the factory, to address the workers. He looked different to the rest, grey yes, but his hair was groomed and his face was harrowing. He was taller but more slender than the others. A black crown signified his authority.

Father recognised him instantly. "That's Cain, the Town's Governor."

"In your world he is, here he leads the Grey Creatures. Cain commands and they destroy." The Labrador told Father.

"He had the last gardens in the town built over and restricted people to one outdoor exercise a day, all so we could focus on work – working for him." Father said angry at the thought. "You know this man?"

"Cain was one of the twelve, like me, he can move between your world and his own realm."

Explained Rafa. "But he turned from our ways, his greedy eyes are fixated only on personal gain. It seems he is not content with crushing nature in your world, he is intent on doing it to mine."

They watched as the Governor gave instructions to the Grey Creatures, he demanded the factory be finished within two days before they moved south of the river. The Creatures set back to work obediently, the noise of the workers starting up again like an engine. Clearly Cain had a great deal of power here, just like back in the town.

"We cannot allow this to happen. Evie is the key…" Rafa began.

But the Golden Labrador was interrupted by thudding footsteps behind them. They turned to see the terrifying image of a Grey Creature staring at them at close quarters.

It swung a huge club towards Father, nearly knocking him over the ridge.

Rafa instantly leapt up and pounced on the fiend, bringing it to the ground.

Father dusted himself off, he had the wind taken out of him and fortunately it was a glancing blow as the fiend's strength was immense. Father was shaken by the experience.

The giant dog growled, bearing his teeth, and told the Grey Creature to stay silent, his huge paw pinning the menace to the ground; he didn't want the other creatures to find them too.

"Why are you doing this?" Father demanded of the beast.

The creature eyed him up and down with cold menacing eyes. "This be our land now. You'll be destroyed like the rest of 'em." It replied in low gruff voice.

Rafa interjected, still on top of the creature. "They have already depleted every resource they had in their own realm, now they will do the same to ours."

Father found a thick branch laying on the ground, picking it up he approached the Grey Creature and studied it warily. He recognised human features (a terrifying thought). It resembled something like a nightmarish Neanderthal. Father raised the branch and brought it crashing down on the creature's head, knocking it unconscious.

"How can Evie stop these monsters without getting hurt? She cannot be put in harm's way." Father said to the Golden Labrador. "I do not care for your prophecy, but I do have an idea. You and I can settle this ourselves, but we need help."

CHAPTER SIX –
THE ASSEMBLY OF THE
ELDERS

Evie was having the most marvellous time living amongst all of the animals in Nineveh, the blue-eyed girl had formed new friendships and learnt a great deal more about nature than she had known before arriving. And that, she decided, was due to actually experiencing this nature for the first time; it was all very well learning about the wildlife that used to exist from her screen time with Father, but she had never dreamed to be able to live and breathe it.

The little girl had been keeping very busy, sowing seeds, planting bulbs and cuttings, and tending to flora.

The Bees were particularly pleased with the flowers she had planted for them. They hummed with pleasure as they took the nectar from the rich purple alliums and pastel yellow roses with divine scents. Evie noticed how each bee collected pollen on their legs ready to move to the next flower, helping to produce even more. In return the buzzing insects let Evie have some of the sweetest honey she had ever tasted.

Later she had comforted an upset mole who had tunnelled too far and mistakenly came up above ground. He couldn't see where he was going and became rather upset.

"Thank you young lady, my eyesight isn't what it used to be." He explained.

The little girl had even helped five lost beaver

cubs find their mother again at the dam.

And of course Mouse would not leave her side, often keeping to the top pocket of her pink jacket whilst poking his face out so he could chat to Evie.

They had formed a bond, both had a passion for life and fun.

All that being so, she was elated to see the boat return with Father and Rafa both safe that evening. Having been apart for so long, the three of them embraced together as a family.

The Labrador Prince called for an assembly of the elder animals immediately – which most annoyed Evie as it didn't include either her or Mouse!

"It's not fair!" She complained to her furry little friend.

Mouse agreed and thought carefully for a moment. "Hang on a minute… follow me!" he squeaked.

Mouse jumped out of her pocket and led the way towards where the assembly was being held in the forest.

"But we aren't allowed..." She protested.

"Don't worry, we aren't going to the meeting of the Elders, I just enjoy climbing tree's, don't you?!" Mouse said with a cheeky grin.

It was nightfall and the stars lit the skyline like tiny candles in the distance. Each Elder sat in a semi-circle in Nineven wooden carved chairs that gleamed amongst the Sycamores. Torches were flickering and the Elders were deep in discussion; Fox, Owl, Badger, Wolf, Bull, Stallion, Doe, Beaver, Hare, and of course Prince Rafa. Standing next to him was Father.

A determined look came across Father's face. He explained what they had encountered on their voyage and even used sticks and stones to draw out a map of the factory on the ground in front of them so all the animals could appreciate his plan.

Father wanted to take the Grey Creatures by surprise, capture Governor Cain and close down the factory. The threat to Nineveh would be over - or so he reasoned. He wasn't really doing this for the animals, but for his daughter; Father believed they could then go home and back to safety. Of course he did not mention this whilst trying to convince the others of his risky venture.

What he had seen had scared Father and in truth he was not sure his plan would work, but they had to try.

"We attack at dawn, silently and as few of us as possible, we must use the element of surprise. Owl will scout ahead from the sky. Hare you are the fastest, you will distract them… here." Father pointed his stick on his makeshift map to where the trees had been felled to the east of the factory entrance.

He then took it in turns choosing each animal for a task based on their skill. "Beaver we need you and your family to build a dam to stop the water wheel turning. The Horses will use vines to pull it down. Bull, you will need to break down the door to let us in…"

"And what will you do, while we animals risk our lives?" Interrupted Fox, clearly sceptical from his tone.

"I will find Cain and put an end to this." Replied Father.

"This is folly and it is dangerous, we should not listen to this *human*." Fox rose from his seat and left.

Father was visibly annoyed; he never did like that fox.

"You must understand Father" Rafa began "Fox has not experienced the most pleasant of lives. He only just made it to Nineveh from your world, but many of his kind were not so fortunate. His family were hunted, ensnared, shot and poisoned by man for generations. He knows what the Grey Creatures are capable of better than most of us."

"Then he would be wise to do something about it. Who is with me?" Father asked hopefully.

Rafa stepped forward from his seat. "I am, always."

The Elders then rose together. "We follow

Prince Rafa!" they declared.

None of them had spotted the two little spies in the trees above them who had been listening carefully as the discussions unfolded.

"They need our help." Whispered Evie to Mouse bravely; a worried look was etched across the girl's face.

CHAPTER SEVEN – THE BATTLE AT THE FACTORY

As they approached in silence the smell of burning and smoke from the factory filled the air. A shiver ran down Father's back. He was still unsure if this would work and how many of them could be hurt. After all this was his plan and his responsibility.

Rafa was by his side though, that gave him confidence.

He tried to turn his thoughts to his beloved daughter and being able to take her home.

As the very first signs of the scarlet sun sluggishly rose, its rays began to seep across the landscape. They could now begin to see the outline of the building. Its chimney was smouldering with a black plume billowing into the air. The grey menaces, obviously do not stop to sleep, Father thought.

Owl had been flying back and forth during the night relaying messages.

They kept still and silent for the most part, crouching down so not to be noticed, to give up their position now would be fatal.

Some of the animal's knees trembled in anticipation of what would come next. The enemy that would face them, they knew, was as fierce as any nightmare.

"Wait for Hare's signal" The Golden Labrador whispered with conviction to the others he could see fear in their eyes.

Rafa had backed Father's plan loyally and in turn the animals were loyal to their Prince.

Then silence, Father could hear his heart beating fast. They waited and waited.

This is taking longer than it should, where was Hare? Had she been captured by the Grey Creatures? Father wondered.

Just then a scurry of legs in the distance broke the silence and a glimpse of a brown tale.

An awful roar thundered in the darkness as the Grey Creatures began one by one to chase after Hare clearing the path for the animals.

"Now, advance!" called Rafa as all the animals and Father moved forward from the woodland.

The charge appeared to move in slow motion.

Up ahead Father could see the horses had made it to the water wheel already; the river had dried up thanks to the beavers' work that night. The dam seemed to be holding.

Bull had sped ahead building up momentum towards the factory door.

But three hulking figures appeared in the dim light, standing in Bull's way. Father knew that the muscular cattle had to break the door down for this to succeed. But he couldn't possibly avoid all three of the menaces. The plan failing at the first hurdle filled Father's mind.

As the three Grey Creatures readied themselves to tackle Bull, a deafening howl erupted behind them, and then in a flurry of white and grey fur, they had been set upon and overwhelmed by the Wolf pack.

Bull spirited forward, lowered his head to point his horns, and eventually crashed through the door. The almighty clatter echoed across the land.

The others raced to catch up and began filtering through the newly made entrance. When Father reached the splintered opening he realised there were more of the menacing Grey Creatures than he had feared and they had already dragged Bull and Stag down (the first of the animals to make it through the battered entrance).

A great snarling furnace lit up the vast room inside and it provided an overwhelming heat.

Chaos ensued. Animals and Creatures fought, their bodies contorting to the flicker of the embers.

Father had a makeshift oak shield which he used to beat his way past one of the creatures, try as he might, he couldn't see Cain anywhere. Stopping him would bring an end to all this destruction Father reasoned – he still didn't know what he would do when he found him.

For the first time since his arrival to Nineveh, Father started coughing again, uncontrollably this time; it was the fumes within the factory filling his lungs.

And then he felt a terrible pain shoot through

his head followed by a throbbing. Father's vision went hazy. He thought he could make out a giant figure looming over him, arms raised. One of the monstrous foes had hit him so hard that he had fallen. "I have failed" he realised and braced himself for the inevitable.

A bark then crackled out and another figure leapt on the oncoming Grey Creature's back bringing it crashing down. It was the Golden Labrador! He had saved Father at the last moment.

As he regained his senses Father could smell burning worse than ever and then what was happening dawned on him. Amongst the carnage, a fire from the furnace was now spreading rapidly through the factory.

Before long Father and the animals found themselves trapped and outnumbered between the fire on one side and twenty or so remaining Grey Creatures on the other blocking the mangled exit of the building.

"What do we do?" asked Bear desperately.

"Did you really think you could stop me?" Hissed a deep voice.

Governor Cain emerged knowingly from behind the creatures smirking. He had been watching the battle from a safe distance it seemed.

The fire was growing and reaching ever closer to the stricken animals and Father.

"It is time to accept your fate, we are the dominant species in these realms." Cain said with pleasure. "Cast them into the flames" he ordered his Grey Creatures.

The animals looked at one another and prepared for the worst. The surprise attack may see the factory burn, but it had come at the cost of their own demise.

The smoke and flames were beginning to intensify, the animals could feel the heat at their backs…

"Leave them alone!" came a familiar voice. Father looked to see Evie and Fox standing beyond the Grey Creatures at the remains of the factory entrance.

Cain turned, surprised to see her, he began laughing "And how do you propose to stop me little girl?!"

"Not just me." Evie responded.

Cain marched towards the girl, his hand outstretched reaching for her.

Fox sprang up to defend her and bit the leader of the Grey Creatures arm, but the giant flung him against the wall and Fox let out a loud yelp.

Cain's eyes now fixed again on Evie and he began to edge nearer. But she stood her ground defiantly as the enemy drew nearer.

A buzzing sound then erupted and with it a dark cloud of thousands of bees rose from behind the girl. They began swirling around the creatures, engulfing each one.

The grey menaces panicked flailing their overgrown arms in desperation. Each one of them turned and fled as fast as they could, Cain amongst them.

Rafa stepped forward "Horse, Owl with me, we need to follow them. Beavers release the dam and put out the fire". The Labrador bellowed, running into the distance.

The animals and Father escaped the burning building just in time, their faces blackened from the smoke. He embraced Evie tightly.

"Careful!" Squeaked Mouse, who was in her top pocket again.

"My darling – you have saved us...as the prophecy predicted... I... I forget how quickly you are growing up." Father confessed, relieved beyond measure.

"We thought you could use the help." Evie said modestly to father.

She then set off running from injured horse to wounded wolf and on to many others, treating them with honey from the bees and other herbal remedies from the forest. Marigold was mixed with Lady's Mantle to treat the wounds that had been suffered. A good number of them owed the girl their lives that day.

Meanwhile the little animals blessed with the

skills to dig, set to work scraping frantically until at last they had widened and redirected the river, flowing again, to consume the flames of the factory. They did not want the fire to spread across Nineveh.

When the flames died down the larger animals and Father used the vines to pull what remained of the building to the ground. And it washed away piece by piece downstream.

"We have done it!" Cheered Evie.

"We could not have done it without you and your friends darling." Father said. "That includes you Fox." He admitted.

Fox nodded and walked away, Cain had injured him and he did not wish to show it to the others.

"Perhaps we will be invited to the next Assembly of the Elders!" Squeaked Mouse, only half-jokingly.

When the smoke had finally dispersed, the morning sun shone brightly and the sound of birdsong echoed out.

The river was clear again and salmon leapt where the dreaded waterwheel had once been.

Evie, Father and the animals mourned their lost friends, celebrated their victory, hugged, danced and sang together – they were finally free. And Evie and Father could now, at last, return home to their family.

The Golden Labrador had been running for miles alongside Horse, whilst Owl soared above them, they kept on the fleeing Grey Creatures' trail which led them to the North Mountains.

They watched the figures slink through the sharp jagged rocks and disappear into the distance. They were still reeling from the bee stings.

Rafa needed to be sure they had left Nineveh for good, beyond the mountains and back to their own realm. He climbed until he could see clearly down to the valley below.

What emerged before him, as far as his eyes could see, were rows upon rows of black tents and around them, thousands of Grey Creatures.

Prince Rafa stood for a while motionless, taking in the sight.

The enemy was not defeated after all. The war on Nineveh, and the nature within it, had only just begun.

Owl landed alongside the Golden Labrador. "We must warn the others. We have underestimated our enemy." Rafa said soberly as they turned to head back down the mountain.

CHAPTER EIGHT - THE FAREWELL

When Nineveh's second moon rose, Evie realised it was time to go home.

The truth of the matter was that she had grown to love this wonderful world and did not wish to leave it. The thought of the gloomy concrete town did not fill her with joy after living amongst the luscious greenery. Moreover the little girl had many new friends.

Although Evie and Father did miss Mother and her Sister Abigail.

Father had insisted that they went back through the gateway as soon as possible – they had tried their best but now, after Rafa had brought back the grave news that the enemy was not defeated, Nineveh was too dangerous. The reports being fed back by the birds were that the Grey Creatures numbers swelled further each day and they were preparing in the North Mountains for an invasion.

So in the days before the moon rose, Father and Evie had helped the animals to organise. They had decided to move their homes to the other side of the river where it was widest so it could become a barrier.

They then went deep into the forest to hide themselves away, hoping the grey creatures would never find them. Some dug huge underground burrows whilst birds built nests only at the very tops of the tallest trees.

Evie sewed hundreds of seeds so that the

animals would have plenty of food. She had even thought to plant extra Juniper trees around their new secret home to help hide them. 'Evergreen camouflage' she called it.

Though it had not occurred to any of them that it was a natural shield that the girl had created and with it the transpiring of the prophecy scroll.

The animals were sad to see them leave. For many of them the prophecy, and the hope that Evie brought, now conflicted with reality. 'Why had it not worked?' they wondered.

Mouse had asked Evie to stay and live with them. But she couldn't, she reluctantly admitted.

"The time has come" said the Golden Labrador that evening, "the moon is at its brightest and its light will guide us to the new gateway."

He then turned to Evie solemnly. "My brave girl, thank you for helping us. However, our situation remains dire. My kind now need me more than you and Father do. I will lead you both to the gateway so that you may return home as I promised your Father, but I must remain in Nineveh."

Evie was shell shocked and tears ran down her cheek, after everything they had been through, she was losing her best friend.

"I understand" she sniffed bravely and cuddled her canine companion. Feeling his soft fur between her fingers.

Then she turned and picked up her green satchel. Many of the animals had given Evie gifts to take home with her which she had packed carefully into the bag. This included the ancient prophecy scroll – the Golden Labrador had declared that fate had moved to ensure that Evie was meant to have it.

Even Father had been presented with a Nineven staff for his bravery at the battle. He kept it strapped to his back proudly. He regretted deeply that they could not help the animals further, but their home (and therefore safety, Father reasoned) awaited them.

They had played their part in a cause that was not their own – he tried to convince himself without much success.

Then, once they had said their goodbyes to their new friends, Evie, Father and the Golden Labrador started their journey back home.

The gateway had moved, it was further north than before. Rafa explained that the position of the moons determine the realm's entrance and exit. "It is a powerful and ancient magic which has, mostly, been forgotten."

Most of the walk was in silence; there was a sense of sadness; an ending. This was the last journey they would have together as a family. This time they stayed close together.

"Just a little further." Rafa said after a while.

Evie's thoughts turned towards home and how different it would seem now. She had grown up so much during her days in Nineveh.

Her daydreams were interrupted by the sound of a branch snapping. The dark cloak of the night sky did not provide much visually, save for the twinkling stars, but the little girl was sure it was neither Father nor Rafa who had stood on a fallen stick.

Then, ahead of them, a hedgeway shook and footsteps could be heard. The three companions stopped.

Rafa sniffed the air, the fur on his back stood up and he let out a deep growl.

Evie could see them now filtering through onto the trail ahead, one after another. They were bigger than she remembered and each of the Grey Creatures emerging before them looked ferocious.

"Out for a night time stroll are we?" Sneered Governor Cain, whose face revealed red sores from the bee stings. "We can't have you breaking curfew."

Evie, Father and Rafa found themselves surrounded.

"My factory is in pieces thanks to you, but no matter, you only delayed our plan, and soon my factories will be everywhere."

Father stepped in front of Evie and Rafa protectively. "Raf you need to take Evie home before the gateway shuts."

The Labrador nodded.

Evie was stunned by the situation they found themselves in. She could only watch as her Father picked her up and placed her on the giant dog's back. Father then reached behind him to hold his new staff aloft preparing to attack.

"How foolish, seize them!" Cain ordered to his menaces.

The Grey Creatures began to the move to towards them.

"Hold on!" Rafa said and Evie instinctively grabbed the mane of his fur.

Father charged forwards and Rafa bolted sideways. Most of the Greys ran towards Father, except one who advanced towards Evie and her Lab. It appeared like a titan rising above them.

The canine Prince broke into a run and then in an unexpected show of strength and agility, leaped high above the creature's head, landed gracefully and ran, never looking back.

But Evie did look, she could see the creatures surrounding her father, and then, he was gone.

The Golden Labrador was still panting and moving swiftly with Evie riding on his back. A shallow stream rippled as they passed through it, it sparkled in the darkness. Small smooth pebbles were displaced by the canine's giant paws; a soft chime sounded out as they knocked together.

Ahead the moonshine met with the trunk of a Maple tree forming an archway like the mouth of a cave. "We need to go back!" She demanded.

"There's no time, the gateway will soon shut." Rafa replied.

He jumped straight through.

The familiar smell of Frankincense filled their nostrils and a blinding white light appeared. To move through a realm gateway was a shock to the system for Evie even if it was the second time she had done so.

Then, presently, they were back where the adventure had started; at the clearing in the Palace wood. The gateway shut tightly behind them.

The little girl and her golden Labrador, who had now returned to his usual size and had lost his crown, looked back despondently. Sadness and disbelief gripped them. They were now just two and were feeling very much alone.

ENDING – A NEW HOPE

The two companions were forlorn and motionless for some time. The air was becoming noticeably hotter as the day wore on. Evie knew they had exhausted the town's laws about allowing daily exercise, but did not care.

Evie suddenly had a feeling they were being watched and then realised someone was in the clearing with them.

She turned around to see the Princess of the Shire standing before them.

Evie gasped and recognised her instantly. Her beauty, emerald green eyes, her long brown locks, her dress and her crown.

"You have come a long way young one." the Princess said in a soothing voice whilst staring deep into Evie's ocean blue eyes, "Yet you have further still to travel on this journey."

"Prince Rafa, despite these troubling times, it is good to see you, it has been a long time." She added.

The dog could no longer speak but he looked at the Princess consciously.

"My Father is trapped back there." Evie finally

managed to say.

The Princess replied, "I know; you will need to go back to him and the others. Take this map it will be as a guide to you."

Evie noticed it was made of the same parchment as the prophecy scroll she had seen in Nineveh. Thankfully it was not in such a decomposed condition and she could make out the drawings.

"And the bearer of this crown will be able to move between each and every realm." The Princess reached up and removed her crown offering it to the little girl. Evie looked at the crown bewildered, only now did she notice that it was made from Nineven wood and adorned with green emeralds. She had always wanted to be a princess after all…

"Time is on your side" the Princess continued, "at least in the right hands it can be."

"But if you are to finish this task that you have started Evie, you cannot do so alone." Explained the Princess "To restore nature, you will need help…"

Later, once the Princess had left them, Evie opened her satchel to place her gifts inside, only to find a stowaway; the little white mouse. He had not left her side and neither had her faithful Golden Labrador.

To Be Continued.

The Hidden Gateway Series will return
in
The Hidden Gateway and the Twelve
Realms

(The first chapter can be found at the back of
this book.)

EPILOGUE

This short story came from an idea about a fantasy adventure which I eventually put on paper during the Coronavirus lockdown – an attempt to be creative for my Daughter; the main character.

The natural world holds different interests for different people, but its essential importance to every one of us should never be underestimated.

Humankind has been destroying wildlife and nature for decades, in 2020 we have now reached a critical point in our history.

The metaphor of the Grey Creatures and the bleak future of the 'town' in the story need not be our own. We can still change our ways before it is too late; we must act to respect and conserve nature, wildlife and the environment.

The Coronavirus crisis has shown that this need for change has perhaps never been more important.

WAYS *YOU* CAN HELP OUR NATURAL WORLD:

- ✓ Respect all wildlife.
- ✓ Create mini nature reserves in your garden – plant seeds, bulbs, flowers and trees of all different kinds. You can even build a small wildlife pond.
- ✓ Encourage pollinators such as bees.
- ✓ Recycle and use alternatives to plastic.
- ✓ Use less energy.
- ✓ Buy sustainable products.
- ✓ Buy organic and free range produce.
- ✓ Become a member of, and/or volunteer for, a wildlife charity.

ABOUT THE AUTHOR

This is the first story that author David Lydiat has written; it is inspired by fantasy adventure books and films he grew up with, combined with a love of wildlife, walks with his family and Labrador, and with nods to Biblical stories.

A family rumour suggests a relation to *Lorna Doone* author R.D Blackmore through his maternal Grandmother.

Concerned by humankind's damaging impact on the natural world, David has volunteered at his local nature reserve in Oxfordshire, the county where he was born and lives.

His background in politics saw him managing successful election campaigns against the odds. This would eventually lead him to Westminster and working for an MP in Parliament for several years. During this time David's roles included speech writing and his accomplished words were etched into Hansard during debates and ministerial questions.

David has regularly read to his young daughter Evie from an early age, establishing a renewed love of books and storytelling. Taken by his daughter's passion for 'story time' he began developing an idea for a tale with Evie as the central character, alongside his old family dog Rafa, who he grew up with.

Evie enjoyed the initial version of the story and thus 'The Hidden Gateway and the Golden Labrador' was born.

Join the mailing list for *The Hidden Gateway* series for free original content and to be kept up-to-date about the latest releases, contact: **lydiatbooks@gmail.com**

ABOUT THE ILLUSTRATOR

Lawrence McClelland is an artist and accountant who lives in York. This is his first foray into illustration during an experimental career. Lawrence has experience using a multitude of media including watercolour, oil, acrylic and enamel paint. Lawrence's drip-paintings have been exhibited in various galleries throughout North Oxfordshire and the surrounding area, which is where the illustrator grew up.

For more information and to view Lawrence's portfolio, please visit **lawrencemcclellandart.co.uk**

The Story continues in the second book:

The Hidden Gateway and the Twelve Realms

By David Lydiat

Available from Amazon or contact
lydiatbooks@gmail.com

The first chapter follows here

Chapter One – The Town

The Princess' words still echoed in her ears as Evie and her Golden Labrador Rafa trudged back through the town towards their home.

"We cannot finish this task alone." The little girl pondered out loud, half expecting her canine companion to respond. "Who could she mean would help us?"

They had spent, what Evie guessed was a fortnight in Nineveh in which her pet Labrador had led them through the hidden gateway in the woods. There he had revealed himself as the Prince of the extraordinary realm where animals could talk and where nature still existed.

However, true to Rafa's words, time had stood still in her own world when they returned and he became mute again.

Though the young girl felt as though she had aged during her time in the other world. And at least they had returned, unlike Father, who's fate at the hands of the wicked Grey Creatures was unknown to them.

Being back in the town after living in the other world felt like falling out of bed during a beautiful dream.

The smog from the factories encircled them, the tower blocks dwarfed them, and the incessant noise drowned them out.

The little blonde girl with the pink jacket still carried her green satchel. With her friend and the precious gifts inside, Evie grasped the bag tightly.

Crowds of people filtered passed one by one from the station like a colony of ants. They were returning from working at the factories.

Evie and the Labrador picked up their pace; amongst these weary, stony faced workers any one of them could be Governor Cain's people.

Cain and his Grey Creatures had tried to capture them as they left Nineveh and she felt it highly likely he would try to do so again here.

Like the Labrador Prince of Nineveh, Cain was a 'Realm Mover', the Crown in her satchel meant she was one now too.

They were just a few streets away from home when Evie caught a stern but pale looking woman with jet black hair from across the road watching them.

Her heart beat faster. Was she being paranoid? Traffic flowed through the gap between them and Evie lost sight of her. "Come on Raf we need to hurry."

The heatwave presented no let up and compounded the inescapable vapours in the atmosphere.

They began to run side by side, Evie looked back... so many people... she began to feel claustrophobic. Her mind raced; what happened to Father? Was he even alive? How would she get a chance to return to him if they were being followed?

Everything was a mess.

Still they ran on, their feet pounding the dirty dark grey streets – much like the colour of those terrible creatures she came face to face with in Nineveh.

Just then Evie's foot gave way, she slipped on rubbish strewn over the pavement and felt a sharp pain in her ankle. Rafa turned to check on the girl, the little white mouse let out an uncomfortable squeak inside her satchel.

As she gathered herself a terrible shiver then ran down her spine, a shadowy figure stood over her blotting out the sun. Out of the corner of her eye Evie saw an outstretched hand coming towards her, to grab her, to take her... Evie could hear her heart thudding inside her chest now and was terrified to look up to the face of who it might be.

Then her dog's tail began to wag happily and she realised it was not a Grey Creature, or Governor Cain or even one of his spies; it was her sister Abigail.

"They are at the house looking for you – the Governor's Agents." She revealed with a concerned frown across her soft face.

Abigail's long brunette locks flowed in the wind. Her teal dress and fondness for violet bracelets added a touch of colour against the grey backdrop.

"We cannot go back there." Evie responded, knowing full well of the reputation of the Governor's people.

"What have you done and where is Father?!" her sister demanded.

"I will explain everything on the way, but we need to leave now. We need to find somewhere safe." Evie said.

"Ok, I know where we can go, follow me." Abigail stated with her usual confidence.

Printed in Great Britain
by Amazon

49356274R00045